Ever After High™

Once Upon a Twist

When the Clock Strikes Cupid

Once Upon a Twist

When the Clock Strikes Cupid

Lisa Shea

New York Boston

Little, Brown and Company
Hachette Book Group
1290 Avenue of the Americas, New York, NY 10104
Visit us at lb-kids.com
everafterhigh.com

First Edition: March 2017

Little, Brown and Company is a division of Hachette Book Group, Inc. The Little, Brown name and logo are trademarks of Hachette Book Group, Inc.

The publisher is not responsible for websites (or their content) that are not owned by the publisher.

Library of Congress Control Number 2016956016

ISBNs: 978-0-316-50187-3 (paperback); 978-0-316-50189-7 (ebook)

Printed in the United States of America

LSC-H

10 9 8 7 6 5 4 3 2 1

For my niece Maria—

you'll always be a princess to me!

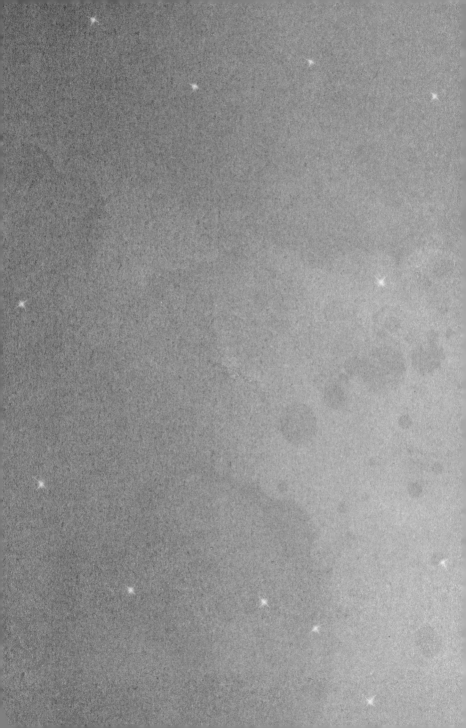

CHAPTER 1

Time for a Change!

Faybelle Thorn was bored. It was a dull day at Ever After High. She wanted to go out and have some fun, but everyone was busy getting ready for midterm hexams. This school year, Headmaster Grimm announced that everyone would have to enter their storybooks and make it to The End of their fairytales in order to pass. This annoyed Faybelle. *Seriously?*

she thought. *You call that a test? I could be the Dark Fairy with my eyes closed.* She tried to convince her fellow cheerhexers to spend the day with her working on a new routine or catching up on their favorite MirrorCast, but they said no. They all wanted to study. Now Faybelle was annoyed times two! She was not used to the fairy cheerhexers saying no to her!

Apple White overheard Faybelle asking the cheerhexers to abandon studying, and she was fairy concerned.

"Faybelle, you should think twice about not studying," Apple said in a serious voice. "It's the midterm hexam! In order to get a good final grade, you have to pass the hexam."

Faybelle just rolled her eyes. Apple was such a goody-goody! *Oh my wand, what is wrong with everybody today? My dull classmates need to get their priorities straight*, she thought.

What could she do to stir things up? Faybelle ran her hand across the storybooks, all neatly labeled and laid out for tomorrow's class. *I should jump into Apple White's storybook and teach her a lesson about being such a goody-goody all the time*, Faybelle thought for a moment. Then Faybelle laughed as she imagined Apple White trying to live *her* life—as if Apple could ever handle being the Dark Fairy. *Wait—now* there's *an idea!* Faybelle knew a way to make her day a lot more hexciting—and everyone else's, too. She would cast a spell and switch up all the storybooks. Everyone would end up in a different fairytale than the one that was part of his or her destiny. *It's perfect*, Faybelle thought. *It will make this hexam fairy, fairy entertaining…for me, at least.*

Whenever Faybelle had an important spell to cast, she had a special way of making it hextra powerful: cheerhexing. She tossed her long blond hair, pulled out her pom-poms, took a deep breath, and gave a cheer:

Study hard and listen well,
As I start to cast my spell!
Whether you're a princess,
prince, or witch,
It's time to get ready for a
great big switch!
S-W-I-T-C-H! SWITCH!

Faybelle did a jump kick and shook her pom-poms in the air to finish her cheer. Then she heard a little *poof!* and she knew that her spell had taken hold. She couldn't wait for tomorrow!

CHAPTER 2

Did Somebody Say Cinderella?

OOOF! Where am I? Cupid thought, gingerly touching the top of her head. She'd fallen into a storybook to take her midterm hexam, but this did *not* look like her story at all. She had been hexpecting to land on top of Mount Olympus, but instead of seeing clouds and bright-blue sky, she was staring up at the roof of a cozy house—probably in a small village somewhere.

As she looked around, Cupid felt hexcited. Had Headmaster Grimm put a special twist on her hexam assignment? Was she supposed to bring love to this little town? *Ooh! That would be spelltacular!* Cupid thought. Then she became aware of a delicious smell. Something fairy yummy was cooking. Peering around the little room, she saw that there was a pot bubbling on the stove and a roaring fireplace in the corner. The smell of the food was making her hungry, and Cupid's stomach rumbled. *Is there a feast about to be served?*

Suddenly, there was a loud banging on the wooden door. A muffled voice shouted something from outside. Before Cupid could answer, a tall woman with pale-blond hair and serious gray eyes and her two grumpy-looking daughters burst through the door.

"Now, I am your stepmother and you should respect me, young lady! When I say supper on the table by seven o'clock, that means you have supper on the table by seven o'clock!" The two daughters nodded in agreement with their mother, hands pressed firmly on their hips. While Stepmother looked disappointed and frustrated, her two daughters looked positively furious! Cupid couldn't understand why they were so upset.

"Just look at her, Prudence," the daughter with short hair said to her sister. "She's just sitting there doing nothing, and meanwhile it's dinnertime."

"Yes, Charlotte. She's being lazy as usual,"

Prudence agreed. "We're all starving! Where's dinner? When are you ever going to get your chores done on time?"

Rather than react to the fact that everyone was being fairy mean for no reason, Cupid did what she always did: She studied the girls to try to figure them out. Part of being Cupid meant really understanding people. How could she help them fall in love if she didn't understand what made them tick? Cupid looked closely at the two sisters. Charlotte had short brown hair, bright-blue eyes, and a sprinkle of freckles across her nose. *She looks like she has a lot of energy. She kind of looks like a gymnast*, Cupid thought. Prudence had long, straight dark hair pulled back in a high ponytail and hazel eyes. *She is probably the quieter sister. She reminds me of a ballerina,* Cupid decided.

The sisters and Stepmother stared at Cupid as they waited for her to respond, but she was too deep in thought, trying to imagine with whom the sisters might fall in love to answer. "We will await our supper in the sitting room," their mother said to Cupid finally. "And you'll finish all your chores...*tonight.*"

Cupid stared blankly at Stepmother and the stepsisters as they strolled out of the kitchen. *Chores?* Well, she'd never thought of bringing people love as a chore, but maybe mortals saw it that way. Cupid reached back to find her bow and arrows—just to make sure they were handy in case a handsome duke or a nice stable boy came by—only to discover they were missing!

Okay, what in Ever After is going on around here? Cupid wondered. Had she lost her bow and arrows? Then she caught sight of her reflection in a mirror. Instead of her usual outfit, she was wearing a dress and an apron. And not a particularly nice dress and apron, either—the dress was old and raggedy, and the apron had quite a few stains on it.

This outfit is definitely not my style, Cupid thought.

But then Cupid replayed everything in her head. Two mean sisters and their mom shouting orders at her about chores...raggedy clothes and an apron...*hmm*...Why did this all sound vaguely familiar?

"Cinderella!" the stepsisters called. "Serve us our dinner this instant!"

Oh. My. Wand. Suddenly, it all made sense—Cupid wasn't on Mount Olympus… because she had landed in Ashlynn Ella's story! In this storybook, she wasn't C.A. Cupid, Olympic Champion of Love. She was *Cinderella*!

Cupid tried to look at the bright side. This could be a little vacation from matchmaking! It had been so demanding this semester at Ever After High. She'd already used more than half her supply of arrows for the year! Now, instead of worrying about practicing her archery skills, Cupid could just sweep some floors, practice her father's angel food cake recipes, and maybe even go to a *ball*! This little mix-up wasn't so bad ever after all.

"Cinderella!" Stepmother barked. "Are you even listening to us? Quit daydreaming and get dinner on the table...*now*!"

"I'll be there in a moment!" Cupid replied.

So long, Cupid—Hello, Cinderella!

CHAPTER 3

Time for Chores

"Cinderella! Cinderella!"

Every time someone called out that name, it took a moment for Cupid to realize they were calling *her*!

"Cinderella! What is all this? What have you done? You usually just serve us porridge in the morning."

Stepmother and the stepsisters stared at the breakfast table. Looking at the spread, it occurred to Cupid that she may have gone a little overboard this morning. First off, there were ten vases overflowing with beautiful, freshly picked flowers in the center of the table. They were almost as bright as the bowls of colorful fruit that sat next to tall stacks of fluffy pancakes and towers of decadent waffles. Then there were steaming-hot dishes of scrambled eggs; sizzling, crispy bacon; and jelly-covered toast. And everything was cut into heart shapes! But suddenly Cupid was nervous. Did she overdo it?

"I—I...just thought it might be fun to have something a little different for a change," Cupid stammered.

"Why is everything a heart?" Prudence asked grumpily as she helped herself to a heart-shaped waffle.

"*Hmm*, well, I started with the pancakes, and then I guess I really got into it!" Cupid said proudly as she watched Prudence stack some heart-shaped bananas and strawberries on her waffle.

"It's definitely different, that's for sure," Charlotte said, heaping bacon and eggs on her plate. "I've never seen scrambled eggs made into heart shapes before."

The faintest glimmer of a smile appeared on Stepmother's face. "Well…hearts mean love. And speaking of love, I believe the prince should be throwing another ball very soon! Charlotte, dear, have you decided which dress you will be wearing?"

"Yes, Mother," Charlotte said. "I decided to go with the yellow one."

"Cinderella, after you have finished all your chores, Charlotte and Prudence will try on their new gowns, and you will alter them accordingly."

"Of course," Cupid replied.

"And, Cinderella...about these pink, heart-shaped pancakes..."

"Yes?" Cupid answered anxiously.

"They're...they're actually not half-bad," Stepmother said. "Please pass me another."

"Sure!" Cupid said with a smile.

So Cupid happily cooked, cleaned, and swept the floor. But after a while her arms started to ache and she realized housework was really difficult without a little magic.

How does Cinderella do it? Cupid wondered, rubbing her arms. Three beds to make up (not even counting her own), the living room and bathroom to keep clean, plus three meals a day for four people. It was simply too much.

"How in Ever After am I going to get through this?" Cupid groaned as she fell back on her bed, hexhausted.

Then she remembered that in the story, Cinderella had helpers! Where were all the cute little critters that always helped Cinderella out? Cupid poked around the entire house until she finally found a family of teeny-tiny doves in their little twig nest on her windowsill. Upon opening the window, the family swooped in and started fluttering about the floor, sweeping up the dust with their little wings.

"You're awfully cute, but you're all so tiny! I'm not sure how much help you will actually be," Cupid told the little doves. But as Cupid went about her chores, the birds followed her.

Much to Cupid's amazement, all the chores went so much faster with just a little hextra assistance. The birds helped her make the beds, helped hang the laundry on the line to dry, and all the while kept up a steady stream of cheerful chirps to keep Cupid smiling while she finished her work.

"We need to get some of you sweeties on Mount Olympus! I think Dad would just *love* having you around!" Cupid said as she blew a kiss to her new feathered friends.

Cupid practically danced through the house, completely enchanted by her nonenchanted chores. She danced all the way into Charlotte's room, sweeping as she went. Trying to reach the tough corner by the back of the bed, Cupid crouched down and saw a pile of clothes hidden under there.

What in Ever After...? she thought as she angled the broomstick to yank out the clothes. *It's fairy strange that Charlotte would be hiding clothes under her bed.* The rest of the room was neat and clean. Right as Cupid was ready to wiggle out the mess, Charlotte stormed in.

"Cinderella! What do you think you're doing here? How dare you enter my room without asking?" Charlotte fumed. Her face was red with anger.

"B-but I was just trying to clean," Cupid started to explain.

"Never ever, *ever* come into my room without checking with me first," Charlotte said sternly. "Now get out of here. And *never* look under my bed again!"

"Okay…I'm sorry, Charlotte. I didn't mean anything by it. I was just trying to make everything sparkly clean," Cupid said meekly, slinking out of the room with her head down.

Cupid felt terrible, as though she had been caught doing something wrong. But had she really done anything wrong? She just wanted to make everyone in this fairytale happy, and she was working as hard as she possibly could—without magic! But even though she prepared everyone's favorite foods and the house was spotless and shining from top to bottom, the stepsisters always seemed to be in bad moods. *Why?*

Cupid didn't have the slightest clue. But she did know that something fairy fishy was going on...and it was her mission to find out what.

CHAPTER 4

Two Grumpy Sisters

That afternoon, Cupid busied herself with cooking up a delicious dinner in the kitchen. Even though she'd started to enjoy cooking almost as much as shooting love arrows, Prudence's and Charlotte's grumpiness still bothered her. Back at Ever After High, she would have talked about it with some of her friends. But she didn't have any friends here. Or did she?

Cupid decided to turn to the feathered friends she had made in this topsy-turvy fairytale.

"Birdies, I'm doing everything I can, and the stepsisters never seem to be happy! Why are they so upset?" Cupid asked.

The birds fluttered around excitedly as they tried desperately to get a message across to Cupid. They wanted to explain what was going on. Finally, one of the birds flew out the door and into the hallway. Cupid chased after him. She found the dove perched on the dining room table with an envelope in his beak. He gently nudged Cupid with the envelope. Cupid opened it up and saw that it was an old invitation to a ball from a couple of weeks past. Cupid looked back at the birds in confusion as they flapped their wings all around the room.

"An invitation to a ball is upsetting to the sisters?" Cupid asked. The little birds all nodded their heads vigorously and twittered in agreement. *But why would an invitation to a ball make the stepsisters unhappy?* Cupid wondered.

Cupid knew she was onto something, she just wasn't sure what it was. So she found a little notebook and started jotting down everything she knew about "her" stepsisters....

After the family enjoyed another one of Cupid's delicious dinners, Stepmother handed Cupid two ball gowns.

"The yellow one is Charlotte's and the purple one is for Prudence," she said. Then she called out, "Girls! Come down here for your fittings!"

The two stepsisters reluctantly trudged over to Cupid. Prudence stepped into her dress. It was beautiful! Cupid couldn't help herself. She gasped.

"Oh, Prudence, this is one of the most hexquisite dresses I've ever seen!" she cried. It looked like Prudence was wrapped in a fluffy lavender cloud. The material was soft and billowy, with satin ribbon trimming puffy sleeves. Tiny sequins were sprinkled all over the dress, so her gown looked like a purple sky full of twinkling stars. It would look amazing in motion!

"Look at my beautiful daughter," said Step-mother proudly.

Cupid stood back and studied Prudence all dressed up. "It doesn't look like this dress needs much altering at all," she said. "It fits you like a dream. Just look."

Prudence stepped in front of the mirror. Before she could stop herself, she shimmied in excitement. Cupid grinned. "I bet the prince will ask you to dance the minute you enter the ballroom," she said. But instead of looking happy, Prudence suddenly turned pale.

"If the dress is fine, Cinderella, please help me get out of it immediately." Cupid didn't understand, but she did as she was told. *If I got to wear a gown like that, I'd never take it off,* Cupid thought, looking down at her own rags.

She let out a little sigh and said, "Okay, Charlotte, you're next."

Charlotte's dress was equally lovely. It was soft, buttery-yellow silk, with lace trimming around the neck and sleeves.

"You look fableous," Cupid told her.

"Yes, yellow always was a good color for you, Charlotte, darling," Stepmother said.

Charlotte studied her reflection thoughtfully. "The dress is fine," she said. But then she made an odd request: "Cinderella, could you make sure it's long enough that my shoes don't show—at all?"

Her mother seemed surprised—and a little bit disappointed. "But, Charlotte, dear,

I bought you a new lovely pair of shoes specifically to match your gown. It would be a shame to cover them up. Look!" And she held up a pair of soft golden slippers with satin bows.

"Mother, please! I don't want my shoes to show! If I can't wear the dress the way I want, I won't go at all!" Charlotte said.

Once again Cupid was confused. The shoes were just beautiful, and she couldn't figure out why Charlotte didn't want to wear them.

Charlotte's mother sighed deeply. "Fine. Cinderella, adjust the gown however she wishes." Then she stared at the shoes in her hands and said, "Maybe I can return these tomorrow." She tried to slip one on her own foot. "I'd keep them for myself, Charlotte, if your feet weren't so very tiny."

Cupid just looked at Charlotte sadly, not saying a word. Finally, Charlotte broke the silence. "You heard my mother, Cinderella!" she demanded. "Lower my hem!" Reluctantly, Cupid did as she was asked.

After she finished both dresses, Cupid took out her notebook and added her notes on Charlotte's and Prudence's strange behavior.

"What is that?" Stepmother asked.

Cupid looked up and hastily closed the book. "Oh, nothing! I'm just—uh—taking notes on Charlotte's and Prudence's dress measurements...what they like and dislike in a ball gown...things like that. It will help me for the next time I need to get dresses ready for them."

As Cupid started to walk to her room, she heard Charlotte calling her name.

"You forgot your book," said Charlotte.

"Oh!" Cupid replied nervously, hoping the stepsister hadn't taken a peek inside. "Thanks, I'll come get it." She started back down the stairs to retrieve it.

"No—wait!" Charlotte said suddenly, and Cupid froze. "Get ready and go long!"

"'Go long'? What does that mean?"

Charlotte laughed. "It just means move back a little," she explained, and so Cupid shuffled up a few steps.

"Now, catch!" Charlotte shouted as she threw the book to Cupid. It landed perfectly in her hands.

"Wow, that's quite an arm you've got there, Charlotte," Cupid observed.

"Thanks," Charlotte replied. And, for the first time since Cupid had arrived, Charlotte's face broke into a big, beautiful smile.

Before she went to bed that night, Cupid decided to bring each stepsister her ball gown. When she got to Prudence's room, she heard a loud thumping sound. She tiptoed to the door and quietly took a peek. Inside, Prudence was dancing around, holding a broomstick. She was trying to dance a waltz with it, but she was so clumsy she kept tripping over her own two feet. *The poor thing,* Cupid thought as she watched Prudence's awkward steps. Prudence attempted a complicated ballroom dance step again and again but kept messing up. She became frustrated and tossed the broom aside. Surprised, Cupid accidently pushed on the door, and it let out a big squeak loud enough for Prudence to catch her watching from the doorway.

"Cinderella! What are you doing there staring at me? Have you been...spying on me?!" she roared.

"No! I didn't mean anything....I was just dropping off your dress...." Cupid tried to explain.

"Get out of here now! You should mind your own business! Stay *out*, Cinderella!" Prudence yelled and slammed the door.

Cupid wasn't bothered by having the door closed in her face because now she had another clue! Hanging Prudence's dress by her door, she quickly made a note in her book.

Pleased with herself, Cupid tucked the notebook back into her apron pocket and headed over to Charlotte's door.

"Come in!" Charlotte called.

Cupid walked in to find Charlotte doing sit-ups on the floor.

"I finished your gown, and I just wanted to give it to you," Cupid said.

Charlotte did another sit-up.

"Thanks. Just put it on the bed," Charlotte said, and continued exercising.

Cupid watched her for a few minutes. "Wow, you're really good at that," she told her. "You must be fairy athletic."

"I am," replied Charlotte, picking up two hand weights. "Speed, strength, and balance. That's what I'm trying to work on."

"That's spelltacular!" Cupid said honestly.

"Thank you," said Charlotte. "I appreciate that. Those three qualities are fairy important to me, if I want to keep my spot on my b—"

"On your what?" Cupid asked. "It's okay. You can tell me."

Charlotte hesitated. For a moment, it looked as if she was going to confide something in Cupid. But then she stopped.

"Why should I tell you?" Charlotte said at last. "It's not like we're not friends. We're not even sisters, really." She looked coldly at Cupid as she spoke. "You're probably just like my mom. All you probably care about is hair, makeup, the Grand Ball, and meeting the prince. Maybe there are more important things—things that matter to me!"

Cupid took a deep breath. "Tell me what *is* important to you! Let's make it happen. I want to help everyone be happy."

Charlotte wasn't convinced. "You want to help me? Really?"

"Yes, of course!" Cupid answered.

"Well, then leave my gown and *get out of here*!"

Cupid gently put the gown on Charlotte's bed and quietly left the room. As soon as she got back to her own room, she made note of everything she had learned about Charlotte.

Later that night, alone in her room, Cupid looked through all her notes. She was starting to get a picture of what made the stepsisters tick....But this was one complicated fairytale! How could she ever put all the pieces together?

CHAPTER 5

Scrub-a-dub-dub

The next morning, Cupid found a thick, creamy envelope with gold lettering at the front door. It was the official invitation from the prince for the Grand Ball that evening! He was throwing the ball in order to find his true love and invited everyone in the kingdom to attend. Cupid was hexcited until Stepmother yanked the invitation out of her hands and told her, "This invitation is not for you."

Now it was Cupid's turn to be upset. She pointed at the invitation. "But...look! It says everyone in the kingdom is invited. *Everyone.* That means me, too!"

"How dare you disagree with me, young lady?" Stepmother yelled. "And anyway, this house is still a mess! You absolutely cannot attend the ball."

Cupid was disappointed. She wanted to see what all the fuss was about. Not to mention, she'd finally get out of the raggedy clothes she'd been wearing all the time. But then she noticed Charlotte and Prudence at the top of the stairs exchanging worried glances. Somehow, they looked more upset than Cupid felt.

The mystery continues, Cupid thought. *What is wrong here? Why don't they want to go to the ball?* She had to find out.

Cupid decided she'd start with Prudence, and this time she knocked very carefully at the door.

"Come in!" Prudence called, and Cupid slipped her head past the door. "Oh," she said, "it's you.... What do you want?"

"Aren't you just so hexcited for the ball?" Cupid asked in her most cheerful voice. "I know you're going to have a fableous time tonight in your beautiful new dress, Prudence."

"Why would I?" Prudence said with a groan as she stood up and walked toward the door. "Tonight will be just like any other night. I'll go the ball, be miserable, come home, and then my mother will blame me for not trying to have a good time. Even if I did try, I still wouldn't be able to do anything right."

Cupid didn't understand what was wrong, and she wanted to help. But before she could say anything at all, Prudence walked out of her room and shut the door behind her.

A short time later, Stepmother told her two daughters to fetch their new gowns; they had to start getting ready right away for the Grand Ball. Immediately, Charlotte and Prudence became sour and cranky, and started barking orders at Cupid to do more chores.

"Cinderella, you have to empty out all the shampoo bottles and wash them, and then pour the shampoo back in the clean bottles. How can I possibly wash my hair with shampoo that's not in a clean shampoo bottle?" Prudence complained.

Just as Cupid finished washing each and every shampoo bottle, Charlotte walked into the bathroom and looked carefully around the room. Cupid couldn't help but get the sense that Charlotte was looking for something to be wrong. Finally, she looked up at the ceiling and smiled triumphantly.

"Cinderella hasn't dusted the ceiling in the bathroom, so how could I possibly do my hair in here?" Charlotte announced, and waltzed out of the bathroom with a dramatic sigh. Cupid quickly grabbed a stepstool and tried to dust the ceiling, but she still wasn't tall enough. Then she remembered her feathered friends! The little birds were happy to help. They flapped their wings across the ceiling. But just as Cupid thought she'd finished with all her chores, Prudence came up with a new one. She wanted the mirror polished. And then Charlotte decided that the bathtub should be cleaned again, even though it was sparkling.

Cupid didn't mind the hextra work, but she did suspect that the stepsisters were making up chores for no good reason. Cupid thought back to Cinderella's fairytale—then she remembered! In the story, the wicked stepmother said Cinderella couldn't go to the ball unless she finished all her chores. The stepmother thought the chores she gave

Cinderella would be impossible to finish, so she would never get to go to the ball!

Then Cupid realized—maybe in *this* story, Charlotte and Prudence were making up these chores so *they* couldn't get ready in time for the ball! Why were the stepsisters so opposed to going to the ball?

Finally, the girls couldn't come up with any more silly chores, so Cupid set to work on getting them ready. She fixed Prudence's long, shiny black hair in an elaborate crown braid. "This looks spelltacular, and you won't have to worry about your hair getting messed up when you dance," she told her. Cupid thought she saw Prudence's eyes light up at the word *dance.* But almost immediately her eyes grew sad again, and her face returned to its usual sour expression. *What can I do to change this story?* Cupid wondered. *I'm not even going to the ball, so how can I help?* Then, she had an idea.

It was time to call for backup.

CHAPTER 6

One Candy-Colored
Coach Coming Up!

Cupid thought more about Ashlynn's story, and she remembered that she should have a fairy godmother to help her. She shut her eyes tightly and wished with all her might for her fairy godmother to appear. When she opened her eyes, Madeline Hatter was there, all dressed up like her fairy godmother!

"Maddie! What are you doing here? This

isn't Wonderland!" Cupid said, surprised to see her friend. Then she gave Maddie a big hug. "You have no idea how 'tea-rrific' it is to see you!

"Oh, hi, Cupid! The Narrators have been telling me all about this topsy-turvy story-book mix-up! All the midterm hexams have been turned upside down by Faybelle. Or maybe they are rightside up. Or sideways? Definitely sideways, like a jamberry upside-down scone!" Maddie said, clapping her hands excitedly.

"So, Faybelle put a spell on the midterm hexams? This is all making so much sense now!" responded Cupid.

"I heard that Cerise Hood and Dexter Charming ended up in Rosabella Beauty's story, of all places," Maddie continued.

"You will never believe what those two are up to...."

As much as Cupid wanted to find out what was going on with her classmates, she also wanted to help the stepsisters. "Can you help me out, Maddie, as my fairy godmother? So far I've been a fairy-fail at figuring out this fairytale."

Maddie laughed. "Of course I can! What you need to do is to throw a tea party and invite everyone!"

Cupid wasn't sure that throwing a tea party sounded like the best solution. How could that help fix the stepsisters' problems?

"Everyone always feels better after a nice cup of tea," Maddie explained. "I'm going to put out my finest tea set. Isn't it spelltacular?

I guarantee this will perk everyone right up! Are there any fresh flowers around here? Help me set the table." Maddie was already putting out her tea set when Cupid suddenly stopped and said, "Wait, Maddie! Can you use fairy magic to make me a horse and carriage, just like in the story?"

"Of course I can. That's easy!" Maddie exclaimed. "Why don't I lend you my teapot for the night? I think it would make a tea-rrific carriage, don't you? And these little doves would make even lovey-dovey-ier horses!"

"Oh, thank you!" Cupid said happily.

"I'll even throw in a wonderlandiful dress for the ball!" added Maddie with a wink.

Maddie waved her fairy godmother wand, and—POOF!—her tea set and Cupid's new critter friends were transformed into horses and a carriage to take Cupid to the ball. And Cupid was transformed as well. The transformation turned out a bit sillier than Cupid expected. Her carriage looked like a giant teapot with four big plates for wheels. It was covered in bright lemon-yellow and orange flowers. Cupid's gown looked like a blue sky covered in pink cotton-candy clouds! Now she had everything she needed to go to the ball.

"*Ohhh*...Cupid! Look at your hair!" Maddie sighed. Cupid peeked in the mirror she had just polished. Her hair was now every color of the rainbow. *This is actually kind of spelltacular!* Cupid thought with a little smile. She twirled in front of the mirror. She loved her new gown! Cupid couldn't wait to go to the ball to see if she could save this fairy topsy-turvy fairytale after all.

CHAPTER 7

Anybody Lose a Sneaker?

Cupid felt like a princess as she walked into the ball. No one recognized her, of course, now that she was out of her Cinderella rags. "You look hexquisite!" one princess said to her as she passed. "*Oooh*, I want rainbow-colored hair, too!" said another. Cupid smiled. The Grand Ball was even more hexciting than she had imagined!

"Excuse me. Would you like to dance?" a young prince asked. He held out his hand to Cupid.

"Oh! Um...maybe a little later. Thank you for asking," Cupid replied.

"I will wait forever for the young lady with the rainbow-colored hair," the prince said.

Cupid watched him walk away and sighed. Maybe if she could solve these stepsisters' problems early, she could enjoy one dance. For someone who was always playing matchmaker and helping other people find love, Cupid never seemed to have any time for romance for herself. Cupid suddenly had an idea. Maybe she could talk about royal balls on her next Mirror-Cast show. She imagined what she would say: *Are you looking for love? Is it your lifelong dream* to meet a handsome prince at a royal ball? Then pay close attention. I'm here to tell you everything you need to know to make a royal hit in romance! Cupid searched the ballroom and spotted the stepsisters moping around, looking even more miserable than usual. *Rule number one: Do not mope around in the corners,* Cupid thought. *You must get out and mingle!* Cupid moved in and watched the stepsisters more closely. She noticed that Charlotte kept tugging at her dress and checking the time. *Rule number two: Always wear clothes that you are comfortable in and make you feel hexquisite.*

Prudence, meanwhile, kept watching the people on the dance floor with a sad look on her face. Then, as Cupid watched, a young prince walked over to Prudence and asked her to dance. Prudence looked surprised and nervous, and quickly shook her head.

"Are you sure?" the young man asked. "Forgive me if I'm being forward, but I couldn't help but notice you standing here by yourself, tapping your foot to the music. I thought surely you would like to dance."

"No...no, thank you," Prudence said firmly.

Cupid looked back to Charlotte, who had moved to a dark corner of the ballroom. *What is she doing?* Cupid wondered. It looked like she was pretending to throw a bookball! *Why would she be pretending to do that? Does she even like bookball?*

A little while later, Cupid went to the bathroom to wash up her hands. When she opened the door, she was surprised to see

Prudence dancing in front of the mirror. She was shimmying and twirling and seemed to be having a great time...all by herself. Luckily, she didn't see Cupid, and Cupid quietly sneaked out, shaking her head. *Why would Prudence refuse to dance with a royal, yet dance alone in the ladies' room?*

As Cupid left the ladies' room, she nearly bumped into Charlotte and her mom. But they didn't recognize Cupid, so they carried on the conversation they'd been having.

"Charlotte. I'm begging you. Just dance with someone. It doesn't have to be a prince. Just dance with anyone. Please," Stepmother pleaded with her daughter.

"Mother, I told you already. I don't feel like dancing right now. If I see someone I want to dance with, I will."

"My dear, you mean to say there's nobody in the entire kingdom that you'd like to dance with right now? Not even a teeny little bit?"

"No, there isn't. Please quit bugging me, Mother. I can't enjoy myself when you upset me like this."

"Oh. Very well, then, Charlotte," her mother said sadly.

Cupid had to admit she was on Team Stepmother here. *These girls just aren't giving the ball a chance!* she thought.

Before long, it was almost midnight. Would the spell wear off like it did in Cinderella's story? Cupid wasn't sure—Maddie hadn't said anything about it. The DJ announced the last dance of the evening. Almost everyone grabbed a partner and started dancing, except

Cupid, who was hiding in a corner, and the stepsisters, who seemed to be hiding, too.

Suddenly, Cupid heard a familiar voice. "Cupid? Is that really you?" She turned around and saw it was Hopper Croakington II! He'd become Prince Charming in this mixed-up fairytale. And it suited him! He was still as nervous and awkward as ever, even though he looked adorable in his Prince Charming outfit.

"Hopper, this is your big chance!" Cupid said. "Why are you hiding in corners instead of tearing up the dance floor? Every princess here would love to dance with you!"

"Maybe, but I'd have to talk to them first!" Hopper said sadly. "And then talk to them some more while we are dancing, and then even more chitchat afterward! I'd just mess everything up, so why even bother?"

"I think you're worrying way too much," Cupid told him calmly. "Hopper, just in case you've forgotten, the only reason these princesses are here is to dance with Prince Charming. And in this fairytale, that just happens to be you!"

"But suppose it doesn't work out, and I change into a frog right in the middle of the dance floor?" Hopper said miserably. "I'd be the laughingstock of the ball! Tomorrow all anyone would be talking and hexting about would be how Prince Charming turned into a frog at his own ball! No, thank you! Better safe than sorry. I'm staying put right here."

But Cupid insisted. "Hopper. Listen to me. I know about *these* things. Dances. Love. Romance. Please—just dance with one princess," she said. "I promise you won't regret it!"

Hopper sighed and scanned the room. He looked just about ready to give up when his gaze landed on one particular princess.

"All right," he said. "I'll ask one girl to dance. Maybe I can give it a shot with that girl over there."

Cupid turned to look at the girl, and then it was Cupid's turn to sigh. It was no surprise that Hopper liked her—she looked like Briar Beauty, and it was common knowledge that Hopper was crushing on Briar.

"That's great!" Cupid said enthusiastically. "So, go over and talk to her. I guarantee you she won't say no."

"Okay," Hopper said. "I *will* ask her to dance! Here I go." He ran his fingers nervously through his hair and smoothed down his jacket. "How do I look?" he asked Cupid tensely.

"Just let me do one thing," Cupid said, and she straightened out his tie. "Now you look perfect," she said. "Fairy, fairy handsome!" Hopper gulped, and glanced again in the direction of the girl. Cupid gave him a little push. "Now go!" she ordered. "Remember to breathe. And have fun!"

Hopper slowly walked toward the girl. His heart was pounding and he was trying to keep calm as he approached her. "Smile. Chat. Pay attention to what she says. Smile. Laugh. Be cool...be cool...be cool..." he told himself. When he was finally next to the girl, her back was to him. He coughed softly and tapped her shoulder. "Ahem!" he said.

The girl turned and opened her eyes wide in shock. "Oh! Your Majesty!" She gasped. She quickly gave a little curtsy. Hopper was immediately uncomfortable.

"Oh please," he said nervously. "There is no need for that. I was just wondering…I mean…do you…would you like…what I'm trying to say…"

Cupid was watching from the corner. "Oh, Hopper," she groaned. "Can't you just relax?" she whispered.

Hopper took another big gulp of air. "Wanna dance?" he blurted out.

The girl gave him a dazzling smile. "I would love to!" she said, and immediately held out her arm.

"Oh! You want me to—I should—well, okay, then," Hopper stammered as he linked arms with her.

Hopper and the lovely girl had been dancing for barely more than a minute when she started complimenting him, just as Cupid knew she would. "Oh, Your Majesty, you are such a spelltacular dancer," she said, smiling up at Hopper.

But Cupid could tell that Hopper was even more nervous.

"Your Majesty, please forgive me, but you suddenly look a little green! Are you all right?" the girl asked. "Do you need to sit down? Can I get you anything? Would you like a glass of water?" She really was being fairy sweet. But it looked like Hopper was getting ready to make his getaway before this girl's prince truly did turn into a frog.

"Sorry. Gotta run," Hopper said, and, much to the girl's dismay, he disappeared.

Hopper rushed over to Cupid. "Whew. That was a close one," he said.

Cupid started to say something, but he stopped her. Hopper held up one hand.

"We had a deal, Cupid. You told me to try dancing with one girl, and I did. You can't say I didn't try."

Cupid agreed. She then realized Hopper could probably use a distraction from the stress of trying to be Prince Charming, and to take his mind off the prospect of dancing with any more princesses.

"Hopper, would you like to help me figure out what my two stepsisters, Prudence and Charlotte, are up to?" she asked.

"Would I? Spying! Wrestling! Anything but *dancing*!" Hopper said, and they both laughed.

But by the time she and Hopper turned to follow the girls, they had already disappeared. Looking out a large window, Cupid spotted the stepsisters' carriage heading away from the castle. Cupid and Hopper ran out the front door and bounded down the stairs toward her teapot carriage. They needed to catch up!

"Cupid, wait!" shouted Hopper from behind her. He had fallen on the stairs. Cupid hurried over to help.

"Are you all right?" Cupid asked, worried. Hopper was okay, but he'd tripped on a shoe—not just any shoe, a red high-top sneaker!

"A sneaker! Oh my fairy godmother! This storybook is getting more confusing by the second. Hopper, what do you think finding a sneaker means?" Cupid asked.

"Somebody wants to be here even less than I do?" Hopper guessed. He shrugged.

But Cupid stood, staring at the sneaker. "Do you think it's a symbol? Or a clue?"

"Maybe it matches the color of the dress of the girl who lost it!" Hopper said. "But I don't know, Cupid; we could be making a big deal out of nothing. Maybe it's a girl who likes sneakers and just wants to be comfortable. I've always been amazed by how you girls can walk around in those uncomfortable-looking, fancy shoes all day—not to mention dancing all night at a ball. Which reminds me: I just want to get out of here. Can we go home now?"

Cupid sighed in hexaustion. "You know, maybe I'll never get out of this storybook," she said to Hopper. "I can't seem to figure out the stepsisters. And now here we are at the Grand Ball, and I don't have a clue as to what's going on, either. What if I can't make it to the Happily Ever After at The End of this story?"

Hopper was shocked. "Cupid, you're one of the smartest people I know," he told her. "And you do one of the most difficult things in the world every day in your 'regular' life. You help everyone fall in love! Do you realize how hard that is? There are so many people in the world who would do anything just to meet that 'special someone,' and you make it happen every day of your life! That takes special skills, a clever brain, and a huge heart. Don't worry, Cupid, we'll figure this out."

Cupid was touched. "That is so sweet of you to say. Thanks, Hopper!" she said. "Okay, let's go home." Together, they headed back to the ballroom to gather Cupid's things. Once they were inside, a colorful, twirling sight caught Cupid's eye. "Wait a sec—is that... isn't that?"

Hopper looked in the same direction as Cupid. Even though the music had stopped, one girl was dancing in the middle of the dance floor. It was...Maddie.

"Hi there!" Maddie said when Hopper and Cupid approached her. "Isn't this ball tea-rrific?"

"Um, yeah it is, I guess. But, um, Maddie, what are you doing here?"

Maddie shrugged. "Well, the invitation said everyone was invited, so I figured, why not?"

"That's great, Maddie, but I think we have to get going now," Cupid replied. "The ball looks like it's over."

Maddie looked disappointed. "Really?"

Cupid nodded. "Really."

Maddie sighed. "Just when things were getting interesting!"

Back at home, Cupid couldn't fall asleep, even though she was fairy tired from the busy night she'd had. After tossing and turning for a while, she decided to go into the kitchen and make herself a cup of tea. She was surprised to see Stepmother sitting at the table.

"Hello, Cinderella," she said quietly. "Can't sleep? Neither could I."

Cupid noticed Stepmother was having tea.

"Yes, I was just going to make myself a cup of tea," Cupid said. "May I join you?"

"Why not?" Stepmother said with a sigh. She scooted over to make room.

When Cupid had her tea in hand, she took a seat next to Stepmother and gently cleared her throat. When Stepmother looked her way, Cupid smiled and said, "I thought my stepsisters looked absolutely lovely tonight."

Stepmother nodded in agreement. "Tell me, Cinderella. Is it wrong for me to want the best for my girls?"

"Of course not," Cupid said. "It's perfectly normal for a mother to want the best for her children."

"That's what I always thought," said Stepmother. "But my daughters seem so unhappy. And they don't like me."

"Of course they like you! They love you!" Cupid cried.

"But they don't. As a matter of fact, most people hate me. Oh, you think I don't hear the whispers? I know all the names people call me. 'Horrible.' 'Mean.' 'Nasty.' 'Wicked,' even."

Cupid suddenly felt a little guilty for thinking a few of those things herself. But that was who she was in the fairytale— wasn't it?

"I just want my girls to be happy, Cinder-ella, that's all. And...that goes for you, too."

"Me?" Now Cupid was really surprised. This didn't seem like the wicked Stepmother.

"Yes, you! I'm sorry I didn't let you go to the ball last night. That was wrong of me. There actually was a girl there that reminded me a lot of you." Here she gave a little laugh. "But her hair was every color of the rainbow. A bit much for a formal ball if you ask me. When I saw her I felt bad, thinking about you sitting here at home, alone. So I'm sorry. And I promise you that the very next ball the prince has, you will be allowed to attend."

Cupid was so shocked, she impulsively jumped up and gave Stepmother a big hug!

Stepmother patted her back and said, "Thank you, dear. I'm feeling much better right now. I think I'll go up to bed."

Stepmother started to walk away and then suddenly stopped and turned back to Cupid.

"And, Cinderella? That heart-shaped meat loaf you made for dinner the other night was simply delicious."

Cupid smiled. "Thank you! I'm glad you enjoyed it."

Cupid went to sleep as well, and later that night she dreamed about sisters, frogs...and meat loaf!

CHAPTER 8

Everybody, Dance Now!

The next morning at breakfast, Cupid brought up the Grand Ball.

"So, how was the ball?" she asked while she served plates. "Did you have fun?"

"It was okay," Prudence said. "The music was good."

"If the music was good, why didn't I see you dancing?" Stepmother cried. "Honestly, Prudence, I just don't understand you."

"Yeah, Prudence, why wouldn't you dance at the ball?" Charlotte asked, helping herself to a heart-shaped waffle.

"What are you talking about, Charlotte?" Prudence said. "I certainly didn't see *you* dancing, either."

"Maybe not, but I wasn't the one tapping my feet in the corner," Charlotte said. "Oh, don't look so shocked. I saw you—everybody saw you! You clearly wanted to dance, so how come every time someone asked you, you refused?"

"I'm…I'm picky? Yes! That's it! I'm picky. I've fairy picky. I'm *soooo* picky," Prudence said nervously, while Charlotte and their mom stared at her in disbelief.

"I don't understand, Prudence. If you wanted to dance, why didn't you just dance?"

"And I don't understand *you*, Charlotte,"
Prudence snapped back. "Why do you even
bother going to a dance if you don't want to
be there?"

"I don't understand either of you girls,"
their mother said with a fairy weary sigh.
"Cinderella, pass me some more of those
heart-shaped scrambled eggs, please."

Later that day, Cupid continued to do her
chores, this time with Maddie by her side.
They talked about Hopper turning into Prince
Charming and the terrible time the sisters
had had at the ball.

"You would think they would be hexcited
about going to a ball and getting to meet a

prince," Cupid said. "But, Maddie, I've never seen two more unhappy-looking girls in my entire life…and I can't figure out *why* they are so unhappy."

Maddie was so excited that she started jumping around as she spoke. "Prudence has two of the same shoe! She's heavy on her toes! She goes left, left, up, down! She's never right! Even when she's right, she's left!" Maddie explained. With that, Cupid was suddenly able to figure out what Maddie was trying to tell her. *Prudence has two left feet—she can't dance!* Cupid smiled. She knew hexactly what to do.

Later that afternoon, Cupid went up to Prudence's room. She was surprised to hear hip-hop music blasting.

"I hate to bother you, Prudence, but I'd like to ask you a favor," Cupid said.

Prudence turned off the music. "I don't even like doing favors for my friends," she replied. "Why would I do one for you?" When Cupid didn't answer, she added, in a slightly less grumpy tone, "Well, out with it. What's the favor anyway?"

"I have a confession to make, but it's a bit embarrassing," Cupid said. "I don't dance fairy well. But I love music, and I love to dance, too! I thought maybe I'd be better with a little practice, but I need a dance partner. And I just heard your music playing as I was passing by your room, and I was wondering if you would like to practice dancing with me?" Cupid hoped her plan would work.

Prudence's face immediately changed. She lost her usual sour expression, and her eyes lit up. "Oh! I love to dance, too," she said. "But I have my own style, and it's not like any of the other girls in the kingdom. When I try to copy the way the other girls dance, I just can't do it. I always feel really awkward and uncomfortable and end up tripping over my own two feet."

"Is that why you didn't dance at the ball?" Cupid asked.

Prudence nodded. "I dread getting asked to dance at the balls, because I know I'm just going to make a fool out of myself. So I always refuse. It's better to stand on the sidelines and watch instead of embarrassing myself, don't you think?"

"Oh my wand! Who told you that you had to dance like everyone else?" Cupid exclaimed. "That's the great thing about dancing: You can just do your own thing and be yourself!" She jumped up and waved her arms in the air and made a funny face. "Crank up that music, and let's both dance the way we *like* to dance—in our own way, in our own styles!"

Prudence smiled happily and put the music back on. Together, they danced around the room like no one was watching—just the way they both wanted. Cupid had never seen Prudence look so happy as she did when she twirled around her room. She was jumping and spinning, and her eyes were sparkling. She had a huge smile on her face.

"I can't believe you can dance like this!" Cupid told her. "You may be the best dancer I've ever seen!"

"Do you really think so?" Prudence asked, stopping for a moment to catch her breath.

"I really mean it," Cupid replied. "You are a fairy good dancer. I love your style! It's spelltacular!"

"Thanks," Prudence said shyly. Then her face lit up into a big smile once again. "You know what, Cinderella? Now I'm actually looking forward to the next ball. I'll just get up and dance and not worry about looking silly!"

"Never be afraid to dance the way you want to—remember, no matter how you dance, it will always be the perfect dance for you," Cupid told her.

"Thanks, Cinderella!" Prudence said.

"Anytime!" Cupid replied.

Yay! That's one stepsister down, only one more to go, Cupid thought. Now she just needed to figure out the deal with Charlotte!

CHAPTER 9

Bookball, Anyone?

Prudence and Cupid danced until they were both hexhausted. They decided to take a little break, and Cupid walked over to the window for some fresh air. She saw a girl sneaking out of the house, looking around nervously. Cupid put her face right up against the glass to get a better look.

"Hey…isn't that Charlotte?" Cupid asked. "Where do you think she's going?"

Prudence rolled her eyes and shrugged her shoulders.

"She looks nervous," Cupid said. "Aren't you the least bit curious about where she's sneaking off to? She's your sister, after all."

Prudence glanced out the window, but it was obvious she wasn't really interested. "I love my sister, but she's a fairy private person—she's always sneaking off places and hiding things in her room. Even though I think we're pretty close, I really have no clue."

"Charlotte doesn't confide in you?" Cupid asked.

Prudence looked sad for a moment. "I wish she would confide in me more. She doesn't allow anybody in her room without her being there—not even me, not even for a second! Like I said, I love my sister, but I really don't know that much about her. It kind of makes me sad sometimes," Prudence admitted.

After a while, Cupid told Prudence she was tired, but she promised they'd practice dancing again tomorrow. Prudence happily agreed, and Cupid left.

As she walked back to her own room, Cupid thought back to the pile of clothes hidden under Charlotte's bed. Fairy strange indeed. Cupid called on Maddie for some help again, and the two of them decided to track down Charlotte. Maddie, as usual, was up for any adventure.

"This is fun." Maddie laughed. "It's so hexciting!"

"Look, there she is!" Cupid said, pointing to a nearby field. They watched Charlotte meet up with some boys from the kingdom who were playing bookball.

One of the boys said, "Charlotte, you're finally here! Come on, let's go!"

"Just give me one minute," Charlotte replied. She started searching through her bookpack for something but came up empty-handed. She looked upset.

Suddenly, Cupid figured it out. She knew exactly what Charlotte was looking for! "Maddie, go find Hopper," she said excitedly. "Bring him to the house right away—I know how we can make this a Happily Ever After for everyone!"

CHAPTER 10

If the Sneaker Fits...

Hopper and Maddie arrived with Hopper's court at the front door. When the formerly wicked Stepmother answered the front door, Hopper's court announced that they were searching the kingdom for the young lady who lost a sneaker at the Grand Ball. Stepmother wanted to make certain the girls looked their best before meeting with the prince. She told the prince and his court to make themselves at home, and then rushed to her daughters' bedrooms.

She found Prudence in her room, music blasting. Prudence was dancing wildly. Her mother shut off the music. Prudence stopped mid–dance move.

"Mother, please!" Prudence said.

"Oh, dearest. Put on one of your prettiest frocks. The prince is here!"

"The prince? What's he doing here?" Prudence peeked out of her bedroom to find the prince and his court in the living room.

"They are looking for a special young lady who left a sneaker at the royal ball. They are trying it on every girl in the kingdom."

"Oh. Well, that's not me." Prudence reached out to turn her music back on, but her mother grabbed her hand and stopped her.

"Prudence. Do you know what this means? If this sneaker fits you, you will marry the prince! Now do put on something pretty, and come downstairs and try. On. That. Sneaker!"

Meanwhile, back in the living room, Cupid stole a glance at Hopper, who looked absolutely miserable. She quietly went over to him. "Hopper, why do you look so down?" she murmured.

"I'm happy to help the stepsisters find their Happily Ever Afters," he said glumly. "But I also know in this fairytale, whomever this sneaker fits is supposed to be my true love."

"That's how the story goes, Hopper."

Hopper looked even more upset. "Yes, but that's *Ashlynn's* story. But it's not mine! I was supposed to meet the girl of my dreams at the ball. She loses her glass slipper or sneaker or flip-flop or whatever. Then I put it on her foot and we live Happily Ever After. Only I didn't dance with anyone last night! I mean, I started to, but then I chickened out and ran away. I didn't fall in love, and I don't want to marry whomever this stupid sneaker fits!"

"Don't worry," Cupid whispered. "I think I know who the sneaker is going to fit. And you're not going to have to marry her, either."

Prudence came down the stairs wearing a pretty blue frock and a sour expression. She did not look happy about having to try on the sneaker. "Oddness gracious, this is ridiculous," she said. "Why would I ever wear sneakers to a Grand Ball under my fancy gown? Who would ever wear sneakers to a ball?" She quickly shoved her foot into the sneaker and waved her foot up in the air. The sneaker was way too small.

"This is a waste of my time," she said. "What am I doing down here trying on sneakers I know don't belong to me when I could be up in my room dancing? Come on, Cinderella, let's go practice," she said. But now it was Cupid's turn to try on the sneaker.

The wicked Stepmother let out a worried gasp, but Cupid said, "I'm pretty sure this isn't going to fit." And sure enough, the sneaker was too narrow for her foot. She stood up, handed the sneaker to Charlotte, and said cheerfully, "You're next, Charlotte!" Charlotte turned even paler than usual. But Cupid gave her a knowing look and a wink. Charlotte slipped it on and laced it up. It fit perfectly!

Prudence was shocked. "That's *your* sneaker, Charlotte?"

"Yes, it's mine," Charlotte whispered. Then she walked over to a table, grabbed her book bag, and pulled out the matching sneaker. She put on both sneakers and stood up.

Hopper looked over at Cupid with wide eyes and mumbled, "Now what?!" He looked frantic. Cupid shook her head and made a gesture with her hand as if to say, *Don't worry!*

Charlotte looked over at her mother nervously. "Mom? Are you angry?" she asked.

The wicked Stepmother screamed. "Oh my wand! My daughter is going to marry Prince Charming! I think I'm going to faint!" And, true to her word, she did.

When Stepmother finally came to, the first thing she did was hug Charlotte. But then she pulled back and saw Charlotte's unhappy face. "Charlotte, my love, whatever is the matter? This is so hexciting! You're going to marry Prince Charming! Why don't you look happy?"

Charlotte took a deep breath. "Mother, I don't want to marry the prince. I never did," she said.

Stepmother said, "Oh dear, I think I'm going to faint...again!" And she did.

CHAPTER 11

The Sweetest Stepmother

Once Charlotte's mother was revived, the first thing she asked was, "Darling, tell me. Why did you wear these sneakers under your beautiful gown to a fancy ball? And why don't you want to marry the prince?"

"It's going to be okay, Charlotte," Cupid said. "Just tell your mom the truth."

Charlotte took a deep breath. "Mother, I'm

sure the prince is fairy nice—" She paused and looked directly at Hopper. "Your Majesty, I'm sure you're fairy nice." Then she turned back to her mother. "But I don't love him, and besides, I'm just not ready to get married," she said. "And as for the sneakers...well, to be perfectly honest, I don't care much for fancy balls. I would much rather be playing bookball with my friends. I'm part of a team with the local boys. I've been sneaking out to play bookball for a few months now." Everyone gasped and waited for Charlotte's mother to explode in anger. But instead, she simply looked surprised.

"Why were you afraid to tell me that?" she asked.

Charlotte was shocked. "Mother, all you

ever talk about are fancy balls and having your daughters marry princes. I thought for sure you'd be furious with me."

The wicked Stepmother then surprised everyone by saying something decidedly un-wicked. "My darling daughter, above every-thing else, I want you to be happy. And if that means playing bookball instead of wearing a ball gown and fancy shoes, then by all means, please, play bookball!"

"Oh, Mother, really? Thank you! Thank you so much!" Charlotte cried, and rushed to give her mother a big hug. It wasn't long before Prudence joined in.

After the group hug, Stepmother looked at Charlotte and asked, "Are you happy now, my dear?"

"Happy? Happy?! *Hexstatic* is more like it!" Charlotte said.

Prudence, meanwhile, had been staring thoughtfully at Hopper. Hopper looked as nervous as ever. But Prudence, never taking her eyes off him, walked right up to Hopper and boldly asked, "Would you please dance with me, Your Majesty?"

"Me…you…dance…now?" Hopper said, stamming. "Well, I…*aah*…you see…" He began to sweat. He felt dizzy. And before he had a chance to run away—*poof!* Just like that, he changed into frog form. But even though he was mortified, Hopper the frog was finally able to find the words to say just what he wanted to. "My dear Prudence, I am but a lowly frog. If you just take a quick look around the kingdom, I am certain there are far better partners for you to dance with than I." Hopper then bowed as grandly as a frog can bow and tried to hop away. But Prudence quickly caught up to him. She picked him up gently and looked him straight in his bulgy frog eyes.

"Wait a spell! I *still* think you would make a fableous dance partner," Prudence said. "I know just what it's like to feel different from everyone else. And you know what? Being different can be pretty spelltacular!"

Hopper the frog couldn't help but smile. A girl—a lovely princess—wanted to dance with him, even when he was a frog!

Prudence put on some music and started dancing. Hopper the frog joined her. He was a little nervous at first, but before long, he loosened up and started having a wonderful time.

"I *loooove* dancing!" Hopper shouted to Prudence. (He had to shout, since she seemed like she was miles above his head.)

"I love dancing, too!" Prudence shouted back. They danced and danced. When the music stopped, there was wild applause.

"Your Majesty, I do believe you should throw another ball right away. I'd love to dance with you on a real dance floor, not just in my living room," Prudence told him.

"I daresay you might be right," Hopper the frog replied.

Chapter 12

A Spell to Remember

Another Grand Ball was quickly scheduled. This time Prudence did not make up any silly chores for Cupid. She was too busy asking for her help getting ready! Then she and Cupid practiced dancing for a little while before they left for the ball.

This time there was no hiding in the shadows for Prudence! She was front and center on the dance floor, twirling happily with Hopper the frog, each dancing to the beat of their own drum. Prudence was jumping and spinning and bopping. Everyone in the kingdom was asking who the wonderful dancer with the long dark hair was. Prudence was a hit!

And nobody had realized that Hopper the frog was actually Prince Charming. They found the frog delightful and charming, and all the girls lined up to take selfies with him with their MirrorPhones. It was one of the best nights of Hopper's life.

Meanwhile, Charlotte was nowhere to be found—at the royal ball, that is. She was outside playing a heated game of bookball with her team while her suddenly not-so-wicked mom cheered her on. Charlotte was laughing and high-fiving her teammates. She spotted her mom in the stands and gave her a huge, happy smile and a wave.

"Woo-hoo! Go Charlotte!" her mom cheered from the bleachers. She nudged the person next to her. "Did you see that? That's my daughter playing out there!" she said proudly.

Cupid and Maddie observed everything going on and then they high-fived, too.

"Prudence is really dancing like there's no tomorrow, and Charlotte is playing bookball with her friends," Maddie said. "That's a Happily Ever After if I ever saw one!"

"It's wonderful and also fairy interesting, too," Cupid said. "This is my first Happily Ever After where love wasn't involved."

"Oh, I don't know about that," Maddie said. "You taught Prudence and Charlotte to love themselves, and that's way more important than falling in love with some boy! And anyway, there is plenty of time for that!"

"You're right," Cupid said. "I think my work here is done."

Maddie agreed as she started to dance. "It's time for us to spellebrate!" she cried, and, just like that, Cupid, Maddie, and Hopper were all on their way back to school.

Back at Ever After High, Cupid's classmates huddled around her, eager to hear all the details of her adventure. Cupid gave her friends and a royally disappointed Faybelle a recap of everything that had happened in her Cinderella story—from the little doves to bookball practice. "It was a bit of a topsy-turvy ending…" she said. "But I can definitely say that we all lived Happily Ever After!"